Samuel Lover

Metrical tales and other poems

Samuel Lover

Metrical tales and other poems

ISBN/EAN: 9783337174385

Printed in Europe, USA, Canada, Australia, Japan

Cover: Foto ©Andreas Hilbeck / pixelio.de

More available books at **www.hansebooks.com**

METRICAL TALES

AND

OTHER POEMS

BY

SAMUEL LOVER

ILLUSTRATED

BY W. HARVEY, HABLOT K. BROWNE, KENNY MEADOWS, F. SKILL,
AND P. SKELTON.

LONDON

HOULSTON AND WRIGHT,

65 PATERNOSTER ROW.

MDCCCLX.

CFTC

A 205320

LONDON:
HENRY VIZETELLY, PRINTER AND ENGRAVER,
GOUGH SQUARE, FLEET STREET.

CONTENTS.

LIST OF ILLUSTRATIONS.

PREFACE.

WE are told of two ladies who sought to outshine each other at every point of rivalry, even to that of dress, and one of them, believing that the gorgeous and the extravagant had been tried *à l'outrance*, determined, on a certain occasion, to try the effect of contrast, and dressed herself accordingly in all the simplicity of white muslin, and by that very simplicity achieved a conquest.

Even so these metrical tales are introduced to society; they affect not the majestic; they do not

> " In scepter'd pall come sweeping by ;"

they do not march in stately Iambic measure, but are content with the easy gait of the Anapestic; they are not gorgeously arrayed, neither weft nor woof of their clothing being of golden thread or Tyrian dye ; in short, like the.lady in muslin, it is on their simplicity alone they must depend for any favour they may win.

It has been said that of late poetry has gone out of fashion; that this is essentially an age of utility ; that amid rapidly-increasing and wonderful realities, the spirit of romance has departed, and fiction has been superseded by the greater wonders of fact.—Poets, however, are a wilful race, and, notwithstanding all the evil forebodings of prosers, would not be gainsaid ; they *would* break a lance in the lists of fame. We have had, accordingly, knights of many new orders : " Satanic "— " Spasmodic "—" Metaphysical "—and so forth ; and now,

" Nobles and heralds, by your leave,"

an old knight of an older order asks permission to run a course for the honour of the lady in white muslin.

But, allegory apart, and to say a few plain words to this so-called prosaic age, the matter of fact is this :—I have great faith in the universal love of rhyme. I think it is inherent in our nature to be pleased with measured sound, and if with measure there is also syllabic echo (I mean rhyme) I think the pleasure is increased; and it is this belief that has tempted me to try the experiment of telling a few simple stories in simple rhyme, and testing if the nineteenth century be not as open as the earlier ones to be pleased with composition something after the fashion of the ancient ballads; and though not adopting their structure as to stanza, and though incapable of equalling the exquisite tenderness in which many of them abound, I have endeavoured to adhere to their unaffected simplicity.

SAMUEL LOVER.

BARNES, LONDON, *November* 1, 1859.

THE FISHERMAN.

THE Fisherman who is the hero of the following tale is not merely a creature of imagination, for the self-denying spirit which forms the staple of the story, is, I am happy to say, in accordance with fact; and the last magnanimous achievement of the poor Fisherman is *literally true*. Magnanimous may seem an inflated word to employ in connection with so humble a subject, but it is believed that the reader, on arriving at the end of the story, will not think the epithet unwarrantable.

THE FISHERMAN.

'T was down by the shore of the steep coast of Kerry

Dwelt a young Irish Fisherman—mournful, or merry,

As the fast-changing flow of his feelings might be ;

Just as tempests of winter will darken the sea,

Or the breeze and the sunshine of summer will chase

In ripples and brightness along its fair face.

And what made the darkness of young Donoghue?

'T was the sense of a sorrow-steeped poverty grew,

Like the dripping sea-weed by the storm-beaten shore,

And clung fast to the heart sorrow's tide had run o'er.

And what made his brightness?   A lovely young girl—

The prize of his fancy—more precious than pearl—

And if diving the sea could have made the boy win it,

Were it fifty miles deep, he 'd have surely been in it.

But parents are thoughtful, as lovers are blind;

And tho' Dermot and Peggy were both of a mind,

The father and mother, on either side, thought

That over-young weddings with sorrow were fraught

To those who were fast bound in poverty's fetter;

So the mother would only consent he should get her

When " times were more promising."   O! where 's the lover

Broke promise so often as Time hath done, ever?

And poor Dermot, as promising periods drew nigher,

Found "Owld Father Time" was a "mighty big liar."

Young Donoghue's friends used to rally him often,

Why to marriage he could not his sweet Peggy soften;

They said, "Marry at once, and take chance, like the rest." [1]

But young Donoghue, while a sigh swelled his breast,

Would laugh off their taunts, and say, "Better to wait

Than 'marry in haste, and repent' when too late."

'T was thus that he *spoke*, but the *thoughts* were more deep

That kept him awake when the world was asleep;

He thought of the joys that would bless him, if she

Were the wife of his bosom—his *cushla ma chree;* [2]

But, suddenly, conscience would sternly reprove,

And balance the scale between passion and love,

[1] See Notes at the end of the Volume.

" By wedding his darlin' what would he be doin'

But playing the guide where the road led to ruin ? "

And then by his manly resolve he would profit,

And, closing his eyes, say—" I must not think of it."

But fancy would trouble his feverish rest,

For in dreams the sweet vision still haunted his breast ;

He saw his beloved one, bewitching, as when,

Fresh, fair, round, and lovely, she tripped down the glen,

Her blush like the morn, and her hair dark as night,

Her brow's playful shadow o'er eyes gleaming bright,

Her lip like the rose, and her neck like the lily,

Her tongue's ready taunt making suitors look silly—

All suitors but one—and to him the sweet tongue

With accents of tenderness ever was strung,

And the eye and the brow forgot coquetry's art,

And were open'd—to let him look into her heart.

O, dream too delicious!—he 'd start and awake,

And again summon courage the dream to forsake—

First, his arms open'd wide to clasp beauties of air,

And then chasten'd thought clasp'd his hands in deep pray'r,

And he vow'd that he never would darken the brow

That glow'd with the light of mirth's witchery now.

And Peggy knew this—and she lov'd him the more;

And oft, when poor Dermot was stretch'd on the shore

And lost in sad thought—pretty Peggy, perchance

Half pleased, and half pitying, might furtively glance

From the cliff overhead—and her sensitive heart

Could divine what his felt—and, with delicate art,

She would gather the flowers from the dark cliff, and pass

Round some pebble a primitive tie of wild grass,

And, attaching her nosegay, would fling it from high,

And the flow'rs fell on Dermot, as though from the sky :—

From the sky ?—say from Heaven :—for the dew ne'er did drop

· From the fountain on high on the summer-scorch'd crop,

More assuaging its fervour, refreshing its might,

Than those flow'rs dropp'd on him from that Heaven-crown'd height !

Then would Dermot take heart—and he thought some fine day

Would reward him, at last, for this cruel delay;

He had heard it remarked, " It was no use to fret,"

And believed there was " great luck in store for him yet;" [3]

And, seeing that nothing is e'er got by wishing,

He thought he'd " get up out o' that," and go fishing;

But even then, Fancy still played her sly part:

The net seemed a woman—each herring a heart.

And thus it went on—weeks and months passed away,

    And Peggy, the pride of the glen,

Grew fairer and fairer with every day,

    And was courted by all sorts of men;

The long, and the short, and the fat, and the lean,

In Peggy's long list of admirers were seen,

But Dermot, in all these great hosts round her thronging,

If he was not the longest, at least was most longing,

Longing—though vista of hope seem'd no clearer,

Longing for time that came never the nearer.

O, longing !—thou love-lure !—with magical art

Engend'ring the sultry mirage of the heart

That flatters while flying, allures to betray,

Exciting the thirst which it cannot allay !

Poor Dermot !—What projects prodigious would start

From the fanciful fumes of that furnace, his heart,

To haunt his poor brain !—Could he seize on some chance

That might better his lot ?—Or his fortune advance

By some feat of great prowess ?—Some high-daring deed ?—

And what danger could daunt him—with Peggy the meed !

Some think we're surrounded by mystical pow'rs,

Who work into shape the wild dreams of lone hours,

And 'twould seem that such spirits were willing to test

The forces of evil and good in the breast

Of the deep-loving dreamer—soon doom'd to a trial

For mortals the hardest of all—self-denial :—

But if spirits of darkness *do* wait, as 'tis said,

To pilot our way, if towards wrong we would tread,

O ! watching us, also, are spirits of light

To shed a bright ray on our pathway when right ! [4]

Now Dermot, as old village chroniclers tell,

Between the two legions was tried pretty well ;—

They both had a pull at him.—Which did prevail

You shall see very soon.—So, to finish my tale :—

One winter's day, when the sea rolled black,

With a fringe of white on its foamy track,

A storm-tost ship by the Skelligs past, [5]

With shattered sail and shiver'd mast;

Vainly she strives to weather the shore—

Brave ship, thy course on the ocean's o'er;

Nor sail, nor helm, nor mariner's might,

Can save thee from being a wreck this night.

The fishermen crowd with coil and rope,

 To the cliff where the doom'd ones drive;

For a while on the earth and the sea was hope,

But nought with the might of the storm could cope—

 'T was a scene that the heart might rive;

The faces of hardy fishermen paled,

And women shrieked, and children wail'd,

While the old village priest lent his hand to the toil,

Heaving the cable and casting the coil,

Cheering his flock with his voice and his blessing,

While deep invocations to Heaven addressing,

And when mortal might could no more essay,

He exhorted his children to kneel and pray. [6]

A sight more solemn was seldom seen,

Than that on the stormy cliff, I ween :

They might not cast down to the sea a rope—

But to Heaven they could raise the holy hope !

And down they knelt in that stormy night ;

The lightning's flash was the altar's light,

And they felt as they knelt on the drenchèd sod,

The thunder, as 'twere the voice of God,

With awful burst and solemn roll

Calling away the sinful soul ;

    And trembling they pray

    For the castaway,

    And many a bead they tell,

As over the billows madly-rolling

The screaming sea-mew circling went,

While the wailing wind was strangely blent

    With the clang of the chapel bell—

Tolling, tolling, solemnly tolling

    The mariners' funeral knell.

When morning dawn'd, the storm was gone,

But the thundering waves kept rolling on ;

And the eyes of the village were set on the sea,

To mark how much of the wreck might be.

Her naked ribs stand gaunt and grim,

While planks and spars in riot swim,

And, among them floating, can Dermot scan

A part of the wreck of the merchantman ;

'T was a laden cask.—The father and son

By a glance implied what might yet be done !

'T was wine—the rich wine of sunny Spain,[7]

If Dermot a cask of that wine could gain,

With the gold he should get for his stormy prize

The dream of his heart he might realise ;

He then might wed Peggy!—The thought and the act

Of the father and son were as one; they track'd

Down the cliff their swift way, and as swiftly their boat

They launch through the foam, on the waves they're afloat—

Have a care how you pull! not a stroke must you miss!

The brave buoyant boat down the wat'ry abyss

Sweeps deeply and swiftly, then up the white crest

Of the wave over-hanging, she lifts her broad breast,

And casts off the foam—like a sea-bird, whose feather

Is made for the storming of hurricane weather.

High heaves the huge wine-cask! they pull might and main,

As near and more near on the waif they gain,

And a coil and a grapple unerringly threw

The hand of the lover—well done, Donoghue!

The cask is secured!—How his heart bounded then!

He 'd have not changed his lot with the proudest of men,

As, lashing his prize to the stern of the boat,

With a heart-wild hurrah Dermot opened his throat,

And then bent his sinewy arm to the oar,

To pull his rich prize where the tide swept on shore ;

But while with fond triumph his bosom beat high,

While hope swell'd his heart and joy flashed in his eye,

He heard o'er the waters a wild wailing cry,

And he hung on the oar with a paralys'd dread :—

For the cry was a cry might have waken'd the dead,

As up rose a fragment of wreck o'er the wave,

Where a man clung for life—o'er a watery grave,

Unless Dermot row back that wild shrieker to save.

With his prize at the stern, he can't row 'gainst the storm,

Where the billows surge up round the drowning man's form.

O ! what shall he do ?—If he cling to his prize,

Then surely that poor shipwreck'd mariner dies.

If the prize he give up—then he loses a wife ;

He then must abandon what's *dearer* than life,—

So he looked to his father, with death on his cheek,

He looked—for in vain had he striven to speak ;

And his father said, " Dermot, my boy, I am old,

I can bear for the rest of my life the keen cold

Of poverty's blast—but for you, darling boy,

With that rich cask of wine, there are long years of joy ;

So do what you like—save the man—*or* the cask—

God forgive me, if answering wrong what you ask."

O ! could you have seen the dark look of despair

Young Donoghue cast on his prize safely there,

While he hears the shrill cry of the fast-sinking sailor,

And pale as his cheek was—just then it grew paler.

Fierce, fierce was the struggle—the foul fiend had nigh

Made Donoghue deaf to the drowning man's cry,

But Heaven heard the short prayer the young fisherman made

To aid him—and swiftly he drew forth his blade,

And the rough-handled knife of a fisherman wrought

A victory more glorious than sword ever fought,

A victory o'er self, and a victory o'er love—

That passion all passions supremely above—

He cut the strong lashings that held his rich prize,

He was deaf to the calls of his own heart's wild cries,

While the cry of another that noble heart heeds—

O ! talk not of laurel-crown'd conquerors' deeds,

Compared with this fisherman's feat of the ocean,

This single-soul'd triumph of Christian devotion !

High Heaven is not slow in rewarding the good ;—

When Dermot the drowning man saved from the flood,

How his heart in its generous virtue grew brave,

When he found 'twas his brother he 'd snatch'd from the wave!

His brother—who long had been absent at sea

In a war-ship, and prize-money plenty made he ;

The money was safe with the agent on shore—

Let the wine-cask be lost in the breakers' wild roar,

As the prize-money freely was shar'd with poor Dermot,

And Hymen gave thirsty young Cupid a permit,

For Peggy was married to brave Donoghue,

The loving, unselfish, and manly and true ;

And, to end, as tales ended in my boyish day,

" If they did n't live happy, that you and I may ! "

FATHER ROACH.

This story, like the foregoing, is founded on fact, and exhibits a trial of patience that one wonders human nature could support. Passive endurance we know is more difficult than active, and that which is recorded in the following tale is strictly true. The main facts were communicated to me many years ago, in the course of one of many pleasant rambles through my native land, by a gentleman of the highest character, whose courtesy and store of anecdote rendered a visit to his house memorable :—I speak of the late Christopher Bellew, Esq., of Mount Bellew, County of Galway.

FATHER ROACH.

FATHER Roach was a good Irish priest,

Who stood in his stocking-feet, six feet, at least.

I don't mean to say he'd six feet in his stockings;

He only had two—so leave off with your mockings—

I know that you think I was making a blunder:

If Paddy says lightning, you think he means thunder:

So I 'll say, in his boots, Father Roach stood to view

A fine comely man, of six feet two.

O, a pattern was he of a true Irish priest,

To carve the big goose at the big wedding feast, [8]

To peel the big *pratie*, and take the big can,

(With a very big picture upon it of " Dan, ") [9]

To pour out the punch for the bridegroom and bride,

Who sat smiling and blushing on either side,

While their health went around—and the innocent glee

Rang merrily under the old roof-tree.

Father Roach had a very big parish,

By the very big name of Knockdundherumdharish,

With plenty of bog, and with plenty of mountain :—

The miles he 'd to travel would throuble you countin'.

The duties were heavy—to go through them all—

Of the wedding and christ'ning, the mass, and sick-call— [10]

Up early, down late, was the good parish pastor :—

Few ponies than his were obliged to go faster.

He'd a big pair o' boots, and a purty big pony,

The boots greased with fat—but the baste was but bony ;

For the pride of the flesh was so far from the pastor,

That the baste thought it manners to copy his master ;

And, in this imitation, the baste, by degrees,

Would sometimes attempt to go down on his knees ;

But in this too-great freedom the Father soon stopp'd him,

With a dig of the spurs—or—if need be—he whopp'd him.

And Father Roach had a very big stick,

Which could make very thin any crowd he found thick ;

In a fair he would rush through the heat of the action,

And scatter, like chaff to the wind, ev'ry faction.

If the *leaders* escaped from the strong holy man,

He made sure to be down on the *heads* of the clan,

And the Blackfoot who courted each foeman's approach,

Faith, 't is hot-foot he'd fly from the stout Father Roach. [1]

Father Roach had a very big mouth,

For the brave broad brogue of the beautiful South;

In saying the mass, sure his fine voice was famous,

It would do your heart good just to hear his " OREMUS,"

Which brought down the broad-shoulder'd boys to their knees,

As *aisy* as winter shakes leaves from the trees:—

But the rude blast of winter could never approach,

The power of the sweet voice of good Father Roach.

Father Roach had a very big heart,

And " a way of his own "—far surpassing all art;

His joke sometimes carried reproof to a clown; [12]

He could chide with a smile :—as the thistle sheds down.

He was simple, tho' sage—he was gentle, yet strong;

When he gave good advice, he ne'er made it too long,

But just roll'd it up like a snowball, and pelted

It into your ear—where, in softness, it melted.

The good Father's heart in its unworldly blindness,

Overflowed with the milk of human kindness,

And he gave it so freely, the wonder was great

That it lasted so long—for, come early or late,

The unfortunate had it. Now some people deem

This milk is so precious, they keep it for cream ;

But that's a mistake—for it spoils by degrees,

And, tho' exquisite milk—it makes very bad cheese.

You will pause to inquire, and with wonder, perchance,

How so many perfections are placed, at a glance

In your view, of a poor Irish priest, who was fed

On potatoes, perhaps, or, at most, griddle bread ; [13]

Who ne'er rode in a coach, and whose simple abode

Was a homely thatched cot, on a wild mountain road ;

To whom dreams of a mitre yet never occurred ;—

I will tell you the cause, then,—and just in *one word*.

Father Roach had a MOTHER, who shed

Round the innocent days of his infant bed,

The influence holy, which early inclin'd

In heavenward direction the boy's gentle mind,

And stamp'd there the lessons its softness could take,

Which, strengthened in manhood, no power could shake :—

In vain might the Demon of Darkness approach

The mother-made virtue of good Father Roach !

Father Roach had a brother beside ;

His mother's own darling—his brother's fond pride ;

Great things were expected from Frank, when the world

Should see his broad banner of talent unfurl'd.

But Fate cut him short—for the murderer's knife

Abridg'd the young days of Frank's innocent life ;

And the mass for *his* soul, was the only approach

To comfort now left for the fond Father Roach.

Father Roach had a penitent grim

Coming, of late, to confession to him ;

He was rank in vice—he was steeped in crime.

The reverend Father, in all his time,

So dark a confession had never known,

As that now made to th' Eternal Throne ;

And when he ask'd was the catalogue o'er,

The sinner replied—" I 've a thrifle more."

" A trifle ?—What mean you, dark sinner, say ?

A trifle ?—Oh, think of your dying day !

A trifle *more ?*—What more dare meet

The terrible eye of the Judgment-seat

Than all I have heard ?—The oath broken,—the theft

Of a poor maiden's honour—'t was all she had left !

Say what have you done that worse could be ?"

He whispered, " Your brother was murdered by me."

" O God !" groan'd the Priest, " but the trial is deep,

My own brother's murder a secret to keep,

And minister here to the murderer of mine——

But not *my* will, oh Father, but *thine !*"

Then the penitent said, " You will not betray ?"

" What I ?—thy confessor ?   Away, away !"

" Of penance, good Father, what cup shall I drink ?"—

" Drink the dregs of thy life—live on, and *think !*"

The hypocrite penitent cunningly found

This means of suppressing suspicion around.

Would the murderer of Frank e'er confess to his brother ? [14]

He, surely, was guiltless ;—it must be some other.

And years roll'd on, and the only record

'Twixt the murderer's hand and the eye of THE LORD,

Was that brother—by rule of his Church decreed

To silent knowledge of guilty deed.

Twenty or more of years pass'd away,

And locks once raven were growing gray,

And some, whom the Father once christen'd, now stood,

In the ripen'd bloom of womanhood,

And held at the font *their* babies' brow

For the holy sign and the sponsor's vow ;

And grandmothers smil'd by their wedded girls ;

But the eyes, once diamond—the teeth, once pearls,

The casket of beauty no longer grace ;

Mem'ry, fond mem'ry alone, might trace

Through the mist of years a dreamy light

Gleaming afar from the gems once bright.

O, Time ! how varied is thy sway

'Twixt beauty's growth and dim decay !

By fine degrees beneath thy hand,

Does latent loveliness expand ;

The coral casket richer grows

 With its second pearly dow'r,

The brilliant eye still brighter glows

 With the maiden's ripening hour :—

So gifted are ye of Time, fair girls,

 But time, while his gifts he deals,

 From the sunken socket the diamond steals,

And takes back to his waves the pearls !

It was just at this time that a man, rather sallow,

Whose cold eye burn'd dim in his features of tallow,

Was seen, at a cross-way, to mark the approach

Of the kind-hearted parish priest, good Father Roach.

A deep salutation he render'd the Father,

Who return'd it but coldly, and seem'd as he'd rather

Avoid the same track ;—so he struck o'er a hill

But the sallow intruder *would* follow him still.

" Father," said he, " as I'm going your way,

A word on the road to your Reverence I'd say.

Of late so entirely I've altered my plan,

Indeed, holy sir, I'm a different man ;

I'm thinking of wedding, and bettering my lot—"

The Father replied, " You had better not."

" Indeed, reverend sir, my wild oats are all sown."

" But perhaps," said the Priest, " they are not yet *grown* :—

" At least, they're not *reap'd*,"—and his look became keener ;

" And ask not a woman to be your gleaner.

You have my advice !"   The Priest strode on,

And silence ensued, as one by one

They pass'd through a deep defile, which wound

Through the lonely hills—and the solemn profound

Of the silence was broken alone by the cranch

Of their hurried tread on some wither'd branch.

The sallow man followed the Priest so fast,

That the setting sun their one shadow cast.

" Why press," said the Priest, " so close to me ?"

The follower answer'd convulsively,

As, gasping and pale, through the hollow he hurried,

" 'Tis here, close by, poor Frank is buried—"

" *What* Frank?" said the Priest—" *What* Frank !" cried the other ;

" Why, he whom I slew—your brother—your brother ! "

" Great God !" cried the Priest—" in Thine own good time,

THOU liftest the veil from the hidden crime.—

Within the confessional, dastard—the seal

Was set on my lips, which might never reveal

What *there* was spoken—but now the sun,

The daylight hears what thine arm hath done, [15]

And now, under Heaven, my arm shall bring,

Thy felon neck to the hempen string !"

Pale was the murd'rer, and paler the Priest.

Oh, Destiny !—rich was indeed thy feast,

In that awful hour !—The victim stood

His own accuser ;—the Pastor good,

Freed from the chain of silence, spoke ;

No more the confessional's terrible yoke

Made him run, neck and neck, with a murderer in peace,

And the villain's life had run out its lease.

The jail, the trial, conviction came,

And honour was given to the poor Priest's name,

Who held, for years, the secret dread,

Of a murderer living—a brother dead,

And still, by the rule of his church compell'd,

The awful mystery in silence held,

Till the murderer himself did the secret broach—

A triumph to justice and Father Roach.

THE BLACKSMITH.

If this story be not founded, like the preceding ones, on fact, at least it has claim to verisimilitude. During the period of " Whiteboy " disturbances in Ireland, special enactments were passed, by which opportunities were but too temptingly afforded to the vicious to implicate the innocent.—Along with this extra legal severity, the ordinary course of justice was set aside ; the law did not wait for its accustomed assizes, but Special Commissions were held, dispensing judgments so fast that the accused had in many cases no time to collect evidence to rebut a charge, and the rapidity with which execution followed judgment utterly paralysed the wholesome agency of respite of sentence. There can be little doubt that the " form and pressure of the time " gave opportunities to scoun-drels to make the oppressive laws of those days subservient to many a base purpose ; and that hundreds of innocent people were transported.

THE BLACKSMITH.

FAINTLY glitters the last red ray,

Tinting the flickering leaves that play

On the swaying boughs of the old gray trees,

That groan as they rock in the fitful breeze.

Deep in their shadow a watcher lies,

The beam of the lynx in his eager eyes;

But twilight darkens—the eye can't mark—

And the ear grows keen to the mental "hark,"

And the rustling leaf is unwelcome o'erhead,

Lest it baffle the sound of the coming tread.

There's a stir in the thicket—a footstep outside,

And the coming one stops in his rapid stride,

As, rising before him, like spectre from tomb,

'T is a *man*—not a *woman*—appears through the gloom,

And he holds hard his breath, and he clinches the hand,

As he halts to the low-muttered summons of "Stand!"

" Who dares to impede me ?"

                           " Who dares to invade

With guilty purpose the quiet glade ?

'T is the brother you meet of the girl you pursue :—

Now give over that chase, or the deed you shall rue !"

" Back, ruffian ! nor venture on me a command !"

And a horsewhip was raised—but the vigorous hand

Of young Phaidrig the blacksmith a blow struck so sure

That it fell'd to the earth the Squireen of Knocklure.

Remember, I pray you, the difference that lies

Between Squire and Squir*een*.   To the former applies

High birth and high feeling ; the latter would ape,

Like the frog in the fable, a loftier shape,

But as little succeeds :—thus are lords aped by flunkies,

And lions by jackals, and mankind by monkies.

Our Squireen was that thing as a " middleman" known,

An agent—the tyrant of lands not his own.

The unscrupulous servant of all who could serve him,

The means of advancement could never unnerve him,

To get up in the world, nothing balked his temerity,

No matter how he might go down to posterity ;

High pay and low pleasures he loved—nothing pure

But pure whiskey could please the Squireen of Knocklure.

The Blacksmith's fair sister had caught his foul eye :

The watchful young brother did quickly descry

The sly-baited lures that were laid to ensnare

Her heart in a hope that might end in despair—

Such hope as too often the maiden enthralls,

Through a villain's false vows, till she trusts and she falls—

So to save from pollution the simple and pure,

Stern warning was giv'n to the knave of Knocklure,

Till Phaidrig, at last, in his passion's fierce glow,

The threat of the horsewhip chastised with a blow.

A vengeance demoniac the Squireen now planned,

In fetters to palsy the brave brother's hand ;

In the dead of the night loaded arms he conceal'd

In the ridge of potatoes in Phaidrig's own field ; [16]

Then the Smith he denounced as a Whiteboy. A search

For the fire-arms conceal'd, tore up many a perch

Of the poor Blacksmith's garden.   What he had intended

Life's prop, was not only uprooted, but blended

With seed of destruction !—The proof-seeking spade

Found the engines of death with the staff of life laid !

'T was enough.—Undeniable proof 't was declared

That Phaidrig in Whiteboy conspiracy shared,

The Blacksmith was seized, fetter'd, sworn 'gainst, and thrown

In a dungeon that echoed his innocent groan.

Those were days when the name of a Whiteboy brought fear

To the passion or judgment—the heart or the ear

Of the bravest and calmest—when Mercy aloof

Stood silent, and babbling suspicion seemed proof.

Then Justice looked more to her sword than her scale,

Then ready unfurled was the transport-ship's sail

To hurry the doom'd beyond respite or hope :— [17]

If their destiny's thread did not end in a rope !

Phaidrig soon was on trial.—When called on to plead

In defence to this charge of a dark lawless deed,

This hiding of arms—he replied, " The Squireen

Showed the place of concealment; no witness has been

To prove he was *told* of the arms being there;

Now how did he know it?   That question is fair—

But unanswer'd.   The old proverb says—' They who hide

Can find.'—'T was the villain himself, who has lied

On the Gospels he kiss'd, that conceal'd the arms there;

My name thro' the country is blameless and fair;

My character's spotless;—Can any one say

I was found among Whiteboys by night or by day?

'T was the Squireen himself who contrived it: my curse

Be upon him this day—for I know there is worse

In his heart, yet to do.   There's an innocent girl

He's hunting to ruin—my heart's dearest pearl

Is that same—and he seeks for my banishment now,

To brand with a darker disgrace *her* young brow;

If I'm sent o'er the sea, she'll be thrown on the world,

Lone, helpless, and starving;—the sail once unfurl'd

That bears me from her and from home far away,

Will leave that poor girl to the villain a prey!

That's the truth, my Lord Judge—before Heaven and men

I am innocent!"—Lowly the murmurs ran then

Round the court; indignation and pity, perchance,

Glowed deep in some bosoms, or gleamed in some glance,

But THE ARMS left the timorous jury no choice;

They found "GUILTY"—and then rose the Judge's mild voice,

"Transportation" the sentence—but softly 't was said—

(Like summer wind waving the grass o'er the dead) [18]

And Phaidrig, though stout, felt his heart's current freeze

When he heard himself banished beyond "the far seas."

"Oh, hang me at once," he exclaimed; "I don't care

For life, now that life leaves me only despair;

In felon chains, far from the land of my birth,

I will envy the dead that sleep cold in the earth!"

He was hurried away, while on many a pale lip

Hung prophecies dark of "that unlucky ship"

That should carry him. " Did n't he ask for his death ?

And sure Heav'n hears the pray'r of the innocent breath.

Since the poor boy 's not *plazed* with the sentence they found,

Maybe God will be good to him—and he 'll be *dhrown'd !* " [19]

Now the villain Squireen had it " all his own way,

Like the bull in the china-shop."   Every day

Saw him richer and richer, and prouder and prouder ;

He began to dress finer, began to talk louder ;

Got places of profit and places of trust ;

And went it *so* fast, that the proverb, " needs must,"

Was whisper'd ; but he, proverbs wise proudly spurning,

Thought his was the road that should ne'er have a turning.

But, " Pride has its fall," is another old saying ;

Retribution *will* come, though her visit delaying ;

Though various the ways of her devious approach,

She 'll come—though her visit be paid in a coach ;

And however disguised be the domino rare,

The mask falls at last—RETRIBUTION IS THERE !

The Squireen lived high, drank champagne ev'ry day,

" Tally ho !" in the morning ; at night, " hip, hurrah !"

In reckless profusion the low rascal revell'd ;

The true " beggar on horseback "—you know where he travell'd.

But riot is costly—with gold it is fed,

And the Squireen's affairs got involved, it is said ;

And time made things worse.   Then, in wild speculation

He plunged, and got deeper.   Next came *pec*-ulation—

There is but one letter in difference—what then ?

If one letter 's no matter, what matter for ten ?

One letter's as good as another—one man

Can write the same name that another man can ;

And the Squireen, *forgetting his own name*, one day

Wrote another man's name,—with a " promise to pay ; "—

All was up with the Squireen—the " Hue and Cry " spread,

With " Five Hundred Reward " on the miscreant's head ;

His last desp'rate chance was a precipitate flight,

In the darkness—his own kindred darkness—of night.

But what of the Blacksmith ?—The exil'd one—cast

From the peace of his home to the wild ocean blast ?

Was he drown'd ?—as the pitying prophecy ran ;

Did he die ?—as was wished by the heart-broken man.

No !   Heaven bade him live, and to witness a sign

Of that warning so terrible—" VENGEANCE IS MINE ! " [20]

He return'd to his home—to that well-beloved spot

Where first he drew breath—his own wild mountain cot.

To that spot had his spirit oft flown o'er the deep

When the soul of the captive found freedom in sleep;

Oh! pleasure too bitterly purchased with pain,

When from fancy-wrought freedom he woke in his chain

To labour in penal restraint all the day,

And pine for his sea-girdled home far away!—

But now 'tis no dream—the last hill is o'erpast,

He sees the thatch'd roof of his cottage, at last,

And the smoke from the old wattled chimney declares

The hearth is unquenched that had burn'd bright for years.

With varied emotion his bosom is swayed,

As his faltering step o'er the threshold 's delayed :—

Shall the face of a stranger now meet him, where once

His presence was hail'd with a mother's fond glance,

With the welcoming kiss of a sister ador'd ?—

A sister!—ah! misery's linked with that word,

For that sister he found—but fast dying.—A boy

Was beside her.—A tremulous flicker of joy

In the deep-sunken eye of the dying one burn'd ;—

Recognition it flash'd on the exile return'd,

But with mingled expression was struggling the flame—

'T was partly affection, and partly 't was shame,

As she falter'd, " Thank God, that I see you once more,

Though there 's more than my death you arrive to deplore :

Yet kiss me, my brother !—Oh, kiss and forgive—

Then welcome be death !—I had rather not live

Now *you* have return'd ;—for 't is better to die

Than linger a living reproach in *your* eye :

And *you 'll* guard the poor orphan—yes, Phaidrig *ma chree*,

Save from ruin my child, though you could not save me.

Do n't think hard of my mem'ry—forgive me the shame

I brought—through a villain's deceit—on our name :—

When the flow'rs o'er my grave the soft summer shall bring,

Then in *your* heart the pale flow'r of pity may spring."

No word she spoke more—and no words utter'd he—

They were choked by his grief ; but he sank on his knee,

And down his pale face the big silent tears roll—

That tribute which misery wrings from the soul,

And he press'd her cold hand, and the last look she gave

Was the sunset of love o'er the gloom of the grave.

The old forge still existed, where, days long ago,

The anvil rang loud to the Smith's lusty blow,

But the blows are less rapid, less vigorous now,

And a gray-haired man wipes labour's damp from his brow.

But he cares for the boy ; who, with love, gives him aid

With his young 'prentice hand in the smithy's small trade,

Whose stock was but scanty ;—and iron, one day,

Being lack'd by the Blacksmith—the boy went his way,

Saying, " Wait for a minute, there 's something I found

Th' other day, that will do for the work, I'll be bound ; "

And he brought back a gun-barrel.—Dark was the look

Of the Blacksmith, as slowly the weapon he took :—

" Where got you this, boy ? " " Just behind the house here ;

It must have been buried for many a year,

For the stock was all rotten, the barrel was rusty——"

" Say no more," said the Smith. Bitter Memory, trusty

As watch-dog that barks at the sight of a foe,

Sprang up at this cursèd memento of woe,

And the hard-sinewed Smith drew his hand o'er his eyes,

And the boy asks him why—but he never replies.

    Hark ! hark !—take heed !

  What rapidly rings down the road ?

    'T is the clattering hoof of a foaming steed,

    And the rider pale is sore in need,

   As he 'lights at the Smith's abode ;

    For the horse has cast a shoe,

And the rider has far to go—

From the gallows he flies,

If o'ertaken, he dies, .

And hard behind is the foe

Tracking him fast, and tracking him sure !

'T is the forger—the scoundrel Squireen of Knocklure !

Flying from justice, he flies to the spot

Where, did justice not strike him, then justice were not :—

As the straw to the whirlpool—the moth to the flame—

Fate beckons her victim to death and to shame !

Wild was the look which the Blacksmith cast,

As his deadliest foe o'er his threshold past,

And hastily ordered a shoe for his horse ;

But Phaidrig stood motionless—pale as a corse,

While the boy, unconscious of cause to hate

(The chosen minister, called by Fate),

Placed the gun in the fire, and the flame he blew

From the rusty barrel to mould a shoe.

Fierce, as the glow of the forge's fire,

Flashed Phaidrig's glances of speechless ire,

As the Squireen, who counted the moments that flew,

Cried, " Quick, fellow, quick, for my horse a shoe !"

But Phaidrig's glances the fiercer grew,

While the fugitive knew not the wreck of that frame,

So handsome once in its youthful fame,

That frame *he* had crush'd with a convict's chain,

That fame *he* had tarnish'd with felon stain.

" And so you forget me ?" the Blacksmith cried.

The voice rolled backward the chilling tide

Of the curdling blood on the villain's heart,

And he heard the sound with a fearful start ;

But, with the strong nerve of the bad and the bold,

He rallied—and pull'd out a purse of gold,

And said, " Of the past it is vain to tell,

Shoe me my horse, and I 'll pay you well."

" Work for you ?—no, never !—unless belike

To rivet your fetters this hand might strike,

Or to drive a nail in your gallows-tree—

That 's the only work you shall have from me—

When you swing, I 'll be loud in the crowd shall hoot you."

" Silence, you dog—or, by Heaven, I'll shoot you !"

And a pistol he drew—but the startled child

Rushed in between, with an outcry wild,

" Do n't shoot—do n't shoot ! oh, master sweet !

The iron is now in the fire to heat,

'T will soon be ready, the horse shall be shod."

The Squireen returned but a curse and a nod,

Nor knew that the base-born child before him

Was his own that a ruined woman bore him ;

And the gun-barrel, too, in that glowing fire,

Was his own—one of those he had hid to conspire

'Gainst the Blacksmith's life; but Heaven decreed

His own should result from the darksome deed,

For the barrel grows red—the charge ignites—

Explodes!—and the guilty Squireen bites

The dust where he falls.   Oh, judgment dread !

His own traitor weapon the death-shot sped,

By his own child it was found, and laid

In the wrong'd one's fire—the gathering shade

Of his doom was completed—Fate's shadows had spread

Like a thunder-cloud o'er his guilty head,

And the thunder burst, and the lightning fell,

Where his dark deeds were done, in the mountain dell.

The pursuit was fast on the hunted Squireen ;

The reeking horse at the forge is seen,

There 's a shout on the hill, there 's a rush down the glen,

And the forge is crowded with arméd men ;

With dying breath, the victim allowed

    The truth of the startling tale

The Blacksmith told to the greedy crowd,

    Who for gold had track'd the trail.

Vain golden hope—vain speed was there ;

The game lay low in his crimson lair !—

To the vengeance of earth no victim was giv'n,

'T was claim'd by the higher tribunal of Heaven !

THE DEW-DROP,

A METRICAL FANTASY.

THE DEW-DROP,

Part I.

A dew-drop, once,

In a summer's night,

Was touched by the wand
    Of a faithless sprite,

As the moon, in her change,
    Shot a trembling ray
Down the bosky dell
    Where the dew-drop lay ;

And tainted with change
    By the wild-wood sprite,
Was the dew-drop, till then
    So pure and so bright.

For what might be pure,
    If 'twere not the dew ?
A gift from the skies
    Earth's sweets to renew.

What may be bright
    As the dew-drops are ?

Kindred are they
>   To the evening star.

Blest is the dew
>   When the day's begun,
It flies to the kiss
>   Of the godlike sun.

Blest is the dew
>   At the evening hour,
Taking its rest
>   In some grateful flower,

That gives forth its odour,
>   To welcome the fall
Of the dew-drop that sinks
>   In the balmy thrall.

Enfolded in fragrance,
>   Entranc'd it lies,

Till the morning's dawn,

When it lightly flies

From the balmy lips

Of the waking flower,

Which droops through the day,

When the dew-drop's away,

And mourns the delay

Of the evening hour.

O, how the sprite-struck

Dew-drop stray'd

'Mong the wildest flow'rs

Of the wild-wood glade !

Toying with all,

She was constant to none ;

Though she held her faith

To the lordly sun.

She sought a new couch
        As the eve grew dim,
But at morning she ever
        Returned to him.

The fond rose pined
        In its hidden heart
While the dew-drop play'd
        Her changeful part.

And though it was kiss'd
        By *some* dew-drop bright,
Griev'd that it was not
        The one of last night.

The leaf-shelter'd lily,
        Pale " flow'r of the vale,"
The love-plaint felt
        Of the nightingale ;

Whose song never bore
    So much meaning as now :—
(), sympathy !—subtile
    In teaching art thou.

The violet (heart-like),
    The sweeter for grief,
Sigh'd forth its balm
    In its own relief ;

While its jealous companions
    Conceiv'd it blest,
And envied the pang
    Of an aching breast.

Thus, eve after eve,
    Did the dew-drop betray
Some leaflet that smiled
    On the pendant spray ;

And blossoms that sprang
    From a healthful root,
Faded in grief,
    And produced no fruit.

But what cared she?
    Who was always caress'd,
As she sank in delight
    On some fresh flower's breast.

Though it died the next night,
    She could pass it, and say,
" Poor thing—'twas my love
    Of yesterday."

At last, in her pride,
    She so faithless got,
She even forsook
    The forgot-me-not.

And Nature frown'd

    On the bright coquette,

And sternly said—

    " I will teach thee yet,

A lesson so hard

    Thou wilt not forget !"

Part II.

The roses of summer

Are past and gone,

And sweet things are dying

One by one;

But autumn is bringing,

    In richer suits,

To match with his sunsets,

    His glowing fruits ;

And the flowers the dew-drop

    Deserted now,

For the richer caress

    Of the clustering bough.

So dainty a dew-drop

    A leaf would not suit,

For her nothing less

    Would suffice, than the fruit.

The bloom of the plum

    And the nect'rine's perfume

Were deserted, in turn,

    A fresh love to assume ;

And, as each she gave up,

    If her conscience *did* preach,

Her ready excuse

    Was the down of the peach.

But fruits will be gathered

    Ere autumn shall close ;

Then, where in her pride

    May the dew-drop repose ?

Nor a bud, nor a flower,

    Nor a leaf is there now ;

They are gone whom she slighted—

    There's nought but the bough.

And the dew-drop would now

    Keep her mansion of air,

With her bright lord the sun,

    Nor, at evening, repair

To the desolate earth ;

Where no lovers remain

But grasses so humble,

And brambles so plain,

So crooked, so knotty,

So jaggèd and bare—

Indeed would the dew

Keep her mansion of air !

But Nature looked dark,

And her mandate gave,

And the autumn dew

Was her winter slave,

When the lordly sun

Had his journey sped,

Far in the south,

Towards ocean's bed ;

And short was the time
    That he held the sky,
His oriflamb waving
    Nor long nor high ;

And the dew-drop lay
    In the dark cold hours,
Embraced by the weeds
    That survived the flowers.

Oh ! chill was her tear,
    As she thought of the night
She had wept in pure joy
    At her rose's delight ;

While now for the morning
    She sigh'd.;—that its ray
Should bear her from loathsome
    Embraces away.

Like a laggard it came ;

    And so briefly it shone,

She scarce reach'd the sky

    Ere her bright lord was gone ;

And downward again

    Among woods was she borne,

To linger in pain

    Till her bright lord's return.

And Nature frown'd

    On the bright coquette,

And again she said—

    " I will teach thee yet,

A lesson so hard

    Thou wilt never forget ! "

Part III.

THROUGH the bare branches

Sigh'd the chill breeze,

As the sun went down

Where the leafless trees

Are darkly standing,

    Like skeletons grim,

'Gainst the fading light

    Of the west, grown dim ;

And colder and colder

    The embers decay

That were glowing red

    With the fire of day,

Till darkness wrapp'd

    In her mantle drear,

The withering forms

    Of the dying year.

Thus bleak and black

    Was the face of the world,

When Winter his silvery

    Banner unfurled,

His sprites sending forth
In their glittering array,
To seize in the night
Each fantastical spray ;

And the fern in the wood,
And the rush by the stream,
Were sparkling with gems
In the morning beam.

So charm'd was the stream
With the beauty around,
That it stopp'd in its course,
And it utter'd no sound ;

In the silent entrancement
Of Winter's embrace,
It sought not to wander
From that charmèd place ;

For better it loved
    With old Winter to be,
In the di'mond-hung woods,
    Than be lost in the sea.

But the dew-drop's home
    Was in yon bright sky,
And when in the sunbeam
    She sought to fly,

Chain'd to a wood
    Was the bright frail thing,
And she might not mount
    On her morning wing.

" Ha ! ha !" laugh'd Nature,
    " I've caught thee now ;
Bride of old Winter,
    Bright thing, art thou !

" Think of how many
    A flower for thee,
Hath wasted its heart
    In despondency.

" Now where thou 'rt fetter'd
    Thou *must* remain ;
Let thy pride rejoice
    In so *bright* a chain."

" True," said the dew-drop,
    " Is all thou 'st told,
My fetters are bright—
    But ah, *so* cold !

" Rather than sparkle
    In diamond chain,
I 'd dwell with the humblest
    Flower again ;

" And never would rove

From a constant bliss,

If I might 'scape

From a fate like this ;

" In glittering misery

Bid me not sleep !

Mother, oh, let me

Melt and weep !

" Weep in the breast

Of my chosen flower,

And for ever renounce

My changeful hour ;

" For tho' to the skies

I shall daily spring,

At the sunrise bright,

On my rainbow wing,

" To my flower I'll return
     At golden even,
With a love refresh'd
     At the fount of heaven ! "

. The Spirit of Spring
     Was listening near ;
The captive dew-drop
     She came to cheer !

Her fetter she broke,
     And the chosen flower
Was given to the dew-drop
     In happy hour.

And, true to her faith,
     Did the dew-drop come,
When the honey-bee,
     With his evening hum,

Was bidding farewell
  To the rose, which he taught,
By his fondness, to know
  'Twas with sweetness fraught.

And the rose thought the bee
  Was a silly thing,
To fly from the dew
  With his heavy wing;

For " Ah," sighed the rose,
  As it hung on the bough,
" Bright dew-drop, there's nothing
  So sweet as thou!"

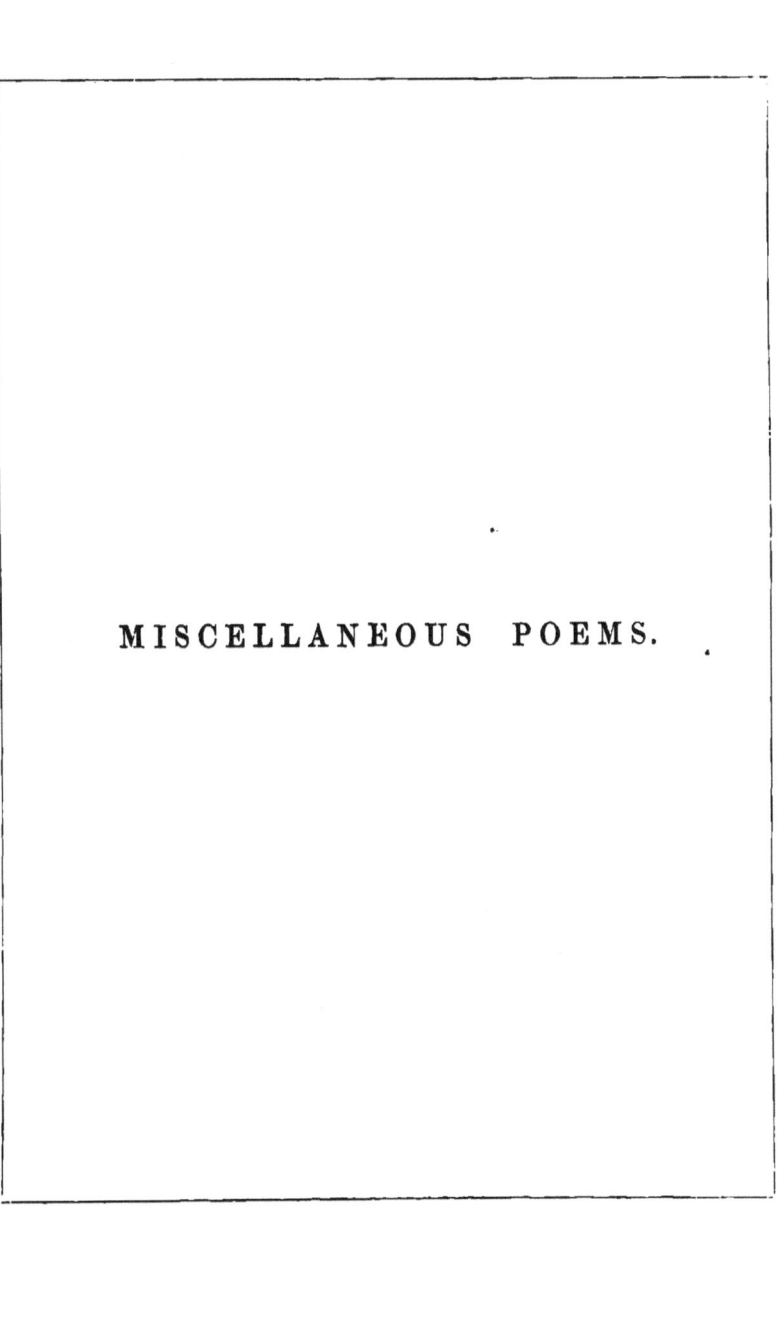

MISCELLANEOUS POEMS.

THE CROOKED STICK.

JULIA was lovely and winning—

    And Julia had lovers in plenty,

They outnumber'd her years

More than twice, it appears—

    She killed fifty before she was twenty.

    Young Harry

    Had asked her to marry ;

    But Julia could never decide,

    Thus early, on being a bride ;

    With such ample choice,

    She would not give her voice,

    In wedlock so soon to be tied ;

And though she liked Hal, thought it better to wait,

Before she would finally fix on her fate ;

For though " Harry was every way worthy " to get her,

Perhaps she might see some one else she liked better.

Hal, discarded by Venus, went over to Mars ;

And set off to the war in a troop of hussars ;

To sabres and bullets exposing a life

Made wretched to him by the want of a wife ;

But Death would not take what fair Julia refused ;

And, in fact, Harry thought himself very ill used

By " Death and the Lady "—till Time's precious ointment,

  Cured the wound Julia made,

  And the soldier's bold blade

Soon won him a colonel's appointment ;

And then he went home, by hard service made sager,

And found Julia had married a yellow old major.

For the sake of old times, Harry called on the lady,

Who was now on *that* side of *this* life they call " shady ;"

Which, though pleasant in streets, in the summer's bright sun,

On life's path is *not* pleasant—when summer 's all done.

He took her hand kindly—and hoped she was well—

And looked with a tender regret on his belle !

" Ah ! Julia ! how 's this ?—I would not give you pain,

But I think I may ask, without being thought vain,

How the girl who refused to let Harry encage her,

Could consent to be trapped by a yellow old major ?"

" Come dine here," said she—" and at evening we 'll take,

On horseback a ride through the hazlewood brake ;

And as I 've lost my whip—you must go to the wood,

And cut me a riding switch handsome and good,

Something nice—such a one as I 'll keep for your sake,

As a token of friendship ; but pray do not make

Your absence too long—for we dine, sharp, at six ;

But you'll see, before then, many beautiful sticks."

Harry went on this mission, to rifle the riches

Of the hazlewood brake—and saw such lovely switches,

But none good enough to present, as a token,

To her who, " lang syne," had his burning heart broken ;

The wood was passed through—and no switch yet selected,

When " six o'clock," suddenly, Hal recollected,

And took out his watch :—but ten minutes to spare—

He employed those ten minutes with scrupulous care,

But, spite of his pains—the best switch he selected

Did not equal, by much, many first he rejected ;

He eye'd it askance—and he bent it—and shook it—

And owned, with a shrug, 'twas a *leetle* bit crooked.

He returned, and told Julia the state of the case,

When she—(a faint smile lighting up a sad face)—

Said, " Harry, your walk through the hazlewood brake

Is my history—a lesson that many might take ;

At first, you saw beautiful sticks by the score,

And hoped to get better, with such ' plenty more,'

But at the last moment—no time left to pick—

You were forced to put up with a crooked stick."

Oh Woman !—designed for the conquest of hearts,

To your own native charms add not too many arts ;

If a poet's quaint rhyme might dare offer advice,

You should be nice all over—but not over-nice.

I don't wish a lady so wondrously quick

As to sharpen her knife for the very first stick ;

But—for one good enough—it were best not o'erlook it,

Lest, in seeking too straight ones—you get but the crooked.

TO MARY.

As in the calmest day the pine-tree gives

    A soft low murmur to the wooing wind,

When other trees are silent—so love lives

    In the close covert of the loftier mind,

        Responding to the gentlest sigh would wake

        Love's answer, and his magic music make.

'Twas thus I woo'd thee—softly and afraid :

    For no rude breath could win response from thee,

Mine own retiring, timid, bashful maid ;

    And hence I dedicate the slender tree

To dearest memories of the tenting fine

I woo'd thee with—as Zephyr woos the pine.

And hence I love with thee through woods to wander,

Whose fairy flowers thy slight foot scarcely bends,

Growing, as time steals o'er us, only fonder,

Following, mayhap, some streamlet as it tends

To a lone lake—full as our hearts, and calm,

O'er which the op'ning summer sheds its balm.

Soft is the breeze ;—so soft—the very lake

Hath not a ripple on its mirror face ;

And hence, a double beauty doth it make,

Another forest in its depths we trace,

The sky 's repeated in reflected kiss :—

So loving hearts can double ev'ry bliss.

The sun is high—we seek refreshing shade,

Beneath the pines we choose a flowery seat;

And, while a whisper in their boughs is made,

Couching, with fondness, at thy tiny feet,

I'll whisper *thee*, while sheltering from the sun—

"Sweet Mary, thus I woo'd thee, thus I won."

THE FLOODED HUT OF THE MISSISSIPPI.

On the wide-rolling river, at eve, set the sun,

And the long-toiling day of the woodman was done,

And he flung down the axe that had felled the huge tree,

And his own little daughter he placed on his knee ;

She looked up, with smiles, at a dovecot o'er head—

Where, circling around, flew the pigeons she fed,

And more fondly the sire clasp'd his child to his breast—

As he kiss'd her—and called her the bird of *his* nest.

The wide-rolling river rose high in the night,

The wide-rolling river, at morn, show'd its might,

For it leap'd o'er its bounds, and invaded the wood

Where the humble abode of the wood-cutter stood.

All was danger around, and no aid was in view,

And higher and higher the wild waters grew,

And the child—looking up at the dovecot in air,

Cried, " Father—oh father, I wish we were there ! "

" My child," said the father, " that dovecot of thine

Should enliven our faith in the Mercy Divine ;

'Twas a dove that brought Noah the sweet branch of peace,

To show him the anger of Heaven did cease :

Then kneel, my lov'd child, by thy fond father's side,

And pray that our hut may in safety abide,

And then, from all fear may our bosoms be proof—

While the dove of the deluge is over our roof." [21]

NYMPH OF NIAGARA,

WRITTEN ON LAKE ONTARIO, IMMEDIATELY AFTER LEAVING THE FALLS.

Nymph of Niagara ! Sprite of the mist !

With a wild magic my brow thou hast kiss'd ;

I am thy slave, and my mistress art thou,

For thy wild kiss of magic is yet on my brow.

I feel it, as first when I knelt before thee,

With thy emerald robe flowing brightly and free,

Fringed with the spray-pearls, and floating in mist—

Thus 'twas my brow with wild magic you kiss'd.

Thine am I still ;—and I 'll never forget

The moment the spell on my spirit was set ;—

Thy chain but a foam-wreath—yet stronger by far
Than the manacle, steel-wrought, for captive of war;

For the steel it will rust, and the war will be o'er,
And the manacled captive be free as before;
While the foam-wreath will bind me for ever to thee!—
I love the enslavement—and would not be free!

Nymph of Niagara, play with the breeze,
Sport with the fawns 'mid the old forest trees;
Blush into rainbows at kiss of the sun,
From the gleam of his dawn till his bright course be run;

I'll not be jealous—for pure is thy sporting,
Heaven-born is all that around thee is courting—
Still will I love thee, sweet Sprite of the mist,
As first when my brow with wild magic you kiss'd!

THE FLOWER OF NIGHT.[1]

THERE is an Indian tree, they say,

    Whose timid flow'r avoids the light,

Concealing thus from tell-tale day

    The beauties it unfolds at night.

So many a thought may hidden lie,

    So sighs unbreath'd by day may be,

Which, freely, 'neath the starry sky

    In secret faith I give to thee :—

      The love that strays

      Thro' pleasure's ways,

Is like the flow'rs that love the light ;

      But love that's deep,

      And faith will keep,

Is like the flow'r that blooms at night.

Then do not blame my careless mien

    Amid this world of maskers gay,

I would not let my heart be seen—

    I wear a mask as well as they.

Ah, who would wish the gay should smile

    At passion too refined for them ?—

And therefore I with blameless guile

    Conceal within my heart the gem :—

      The love that strays

      Thro' pleasure's ways,

Is like the flow'rs that love the light ;

      But love that's deep,

      And faith will keep,

Is like the flow'r that blooms at night.

THE FORSAKEN.

LET us talk of grief no more
   Till the bat is flying;
Fitter mem'ry's sadd'ning lore
   When the day is dying,
When the joyous sun hath fled,
And weeping dews around are shed:
Sad things are most fitly said,
   When the night wind's sighing.

Sighing round some lonely tow'r
   Where, within, is mourning;
And on the hearth, at midnight hour,
   Low the brands are burning.
There the embers, fading fast,
(Relics of a glowing past)
Tell of fires too fierce to last :—
   Love knows no returning.

YEARNING.

Far shore, far shore—*how* far

   O'er the tide of Time you seem ;—

Where is the mystic star

To guide o'er the waters far—

   To that shore of my fancy's dream ?

Far shore, far shore, on thee

   Are the flowers in endless bloom ?

Or there may the desert bo,

With the deadly Upas tree,

   Where the seeker but finds a tomb ?

A voice from the deep replied—

    " Ask not what lies before—

(Vain wish, by Heaven denied ;)

Thy bark a resistless tide

    Will bear, as it others bore.

" Dream not of shores so far,

    Heed not a siren's song,

Seek not for mystic star—

Trust to the means that are—

    Be thy voyage or short, or long."

LOVE AND DEATH,

A FABLE FROM ÆSOP.

VERSIFIED AND DI-VERSIFIED.

Cupid, one day, was surprised in a shower of rain,

(He's a delicate fellow);

So, for shelter, he ran to a shadowy grotto hard by,

    For he had no umbrella.

He thought he might rest while the storm was in action, so he

    Lapp'd one wing o'er his head,

The other he folded so nicely beneath him, and slept

    On his own feather bed.

Oh Cupid ! you stupid, what were you about

    To lie down in that cave ?—

    'Twas as good as a grave—

    As he soon found out.

For the arch where the Archer reposed was the cavern of Death,

    Who had stol'n out, unknown,

To unfasten the portals of life with his *skeleton* keys,

    In St. Mary-le-*bone*.

Soon he returned, and Love, waking, to see the grim king

    With terror did shiver,

And, in a hurry arising, his arrows he dropt

In a *quake* from his *quiver.*

Oh Cupid ! you stupid, 'twas silly to fly ;

Death could not hurt you :—

For love, when 'tis true,

It never can die !

Now the arrows of Death were all lying about on the ground,

And with Cupid's did mix,

And, ever since, Cupid and Death are unconsciously playing

Most unlucky tricks ;

For Love, having gather'd some arrows of Death with his own,

Sometimes makes a hit

At the " *gallery* of beauty," but finds that his mistaken shaft

Drives some belle to " *the pit.*"

Oh! Cupid, you stupid, why spoil thus your quiver,

And send to the *heart*

Some poisonous dart,

That was meant for the *liver ?*

And Death, as unconsciously shooting Love's arrows around,

To bring down the old ones,

Sees grandads and dowagers wondrously *warm'd* into love,

That he meant to be *cold* ones.

Oh! mischievous medley of Love and of Death :—which is worse—

('T is a question perplexing ;—)

To be too young to die, or be too old to love ?—both perverse,

Are confoundedly vexing.

Oh Cupid !—how sadly grotesque is the view

Of white gloves and favours

To Death, for his labours,

And hat-bands to you !

NOTES.

NOTES.

— • —

THE FISHERMAN.

Note 1—Page 13.

Marry at once, and take chance like the rest.

The improvidence of the Irish in their early marriages has been often made the subject of indiscriminate censure by writers who are only too willing to find fault with poor Pat, and either overlook or will not see any countervailing argument in his favour. That improvident marriages often lead to distress cannot be denied, but let it be remembered, at the same time, that they prevent what is worse than distress;—crime. Parliamentary inquiry has proved that crime of the particular character to which allusion is here made, is more rare in Ireland than in any other part of the kingdom—perhaps it may be said, than in any other part of the world: and while using the general term "crime," it must be remembered that there are many branches of it, the branches much worse, by the by, than the main offence; for the first crime is consistent, at least, with humanity, though it is humanity under the penalty

of the fall, while the after crimes are abhorrent to our nature. The daily Police
Reports of England give such melancholy evidence of a criminal state of
society on this point, that, in comparison, the improvident marriages of Ireland
may be looked upon as beneficial rather than censurable.—A quotation from
the leviathan journal of London will form an appropriate conclusion to this
note, and offer a strong argument in its support. In an article touching one
of our statistical tables, (I think a report of the Registrar-General) this
passage occurs :—"There cannot be a worse indication of a people's social
state than the decay or neglect of the marriage institution. The home and
the family are at the bottom of all national virtues, and if these foundations
of good citizenship are impaired, the whole superstructure is in danger."—
The Times, September 28, 1859.

Note 2—Page 13.

Cushla ma chree.

It would be hard to find a more touching term of endearment than this,
" vein of my heart." The true spelling in the Celtic is *chuisle mo chroidhe ;* but
the vulgar spelling may be considered pardonable, if not preferable, in familiar
usage.

Note 3—Page 17.

He had heard it remarked, " It was no use to fret,"
And believed there was " great luck in store for him yet."

There is something very touching in the hopefulness of the Irish peasantry,
in the midst of all their poverty and other trials; and the two sayings quoted

above, are frequently heard amongst this light-hearted people. As to Pat's aspirations for luck, he is accused of sometimes making a blunder in giving them expression, when he crowns a cup to Fortune, and exclaims "The worse luck now, the *more* another time!"

Note 4—Page 19.

Some think we're surrounded by mystical pow'rs,

But if spirits of darkness do wait, as 't is said,
To pilot our way, if towards wrong we would tread,
O! watching us, also, are spirits of light,
To shed a bright ray on our pathway when right!

How prevalent this belief in attendant spirits has ever been, and still is, we have proof from the earliest times to our own. And this belief is no proof of a weak mind, for one of the greatest philosophers of antiquity held it: Socrates had his demon. Nor is the belief confined to Paganism, for a Christian of high mental power has recorded a similar credence. Alexander Pope thus writes to a friend: "Like the trust we have in benevolent spirits, who, though we never see or hear them, we think are constantly praying for us." And this passage Doctor Johnson has quoted in his dictionary, the Doctor himself sharing in the belief with Pope. But, to go to the highest authority, is it not recorded in Holy Writ that the harp of David was employed to charm away the evil spirit that made terrible the dark hour of Saul?

Note 5—Page 19.

A storm-tost ship by the Skelligs past!

Those bold masses of rock, standing some miles from the coast of Kerry, rise abruptly from the sea at so acute an angle as to resemble a double obelisk or acute pyramid, in some views, and hence are looked for as a landmark by mariners. The point is of such importance to seafarers, that a lighthouse is established here, and therefore many a ship, storm-tossed or otherwise, passes the Skelligs, where so heavy a sea runs in general, that the lighthouse has to be well furnished with supplies of provisions, as sometimes, for six consecutive weeks, it is impossible for any craft to approach the solitary landing-place on these desolate crags.

Note 6—Page 20.

He exhorted his children to kneel and pray.

This is not an imaginary incident. Just such a scene was witnessed by a friend of mine, who communicated this fact to me many years ago, and it made too deep an impression on my memory ever to be forgotten.

Note 7—Page 22.

'Twas wine—the rich wine of sunny Spain!

How they should know this cask contained wine, and not only wine, but pronounced to be the wine of Spain, may seem a stretch of the author's imagination, or that too much is assumed for the acuteness of his fellow-countrymen;

but the inference of the fishermen will be acknowledged as perfectly natural, when it is stated that a mercantile intercourse between Spain and Galway has existed for a very long time, and that along the western coast of Ireland, that fact is perfectly well understood; but many a cast-away cask of wine, before and since O'Donoghue's day, might have enlightened stupider fellows than Irish fishermen are in general, without any special knowledge of Galway importations.

FATHER ROACH.

NOTE 8—Page 32.

To carve the big goose at the big wedding feast.

The festivities attendant on the rustic wedding in Ireland are never considered complete without the presence of the priest, who holds presidential authority.

NOTE 9—Page 32.

With a very big picture upon it of " Dan."

" Dan " signifies Daniel O'Connell, whose portraits, in the times alluded to, abounded throughout the length and breadth of the kingdom, and in Ireland very generally on drinking vessels. The above diminutive of his potent name, was that by which the peasantry of Ireland loved to designate him. It was short, and could pass the more rapidly from lip to lip of the people whose principal theme of conversation he constituted; and as they loved as well as honoured him, the familiarity of the term was more consonant with affection. It may be generally remarked, that great men are seldom designated in public parlance by their proper names. The great Napoleon was familiarly known to the French army under the title of "The Little Corporal." The great English Admiral, Lord St. Vincent, was called "Billy Blue" in the fleet; and the illustrious Irishman, Wellington, was endeared to his soldiers under the significant and rather comical nickname of "Nosey."

Note 10—Page 32.

" The miles he'd to travel would throuble you countin'.
The duties were heavy—to go through them all—
Of the wedding, the christ'ning, the mass, and sick call."

This is not an overdrawn picture. In some of the wild districts of Ireland, the duties of the Roman Catholic priesthood are very onerous.

Note 11—Page 33.

And the Blackfoot who courted each foeman's approach !
Faith, 't is hotfoot he'd fly from the stout Father Roach.

"Blackfoot" was the name of one of the many factions that disturbed public peace in Ireland some forty years ago; and "hotfoot" is an Hibernian figure of speech denoting quick walking or running.

Note 12—Page 34.

And " a way of his own"—far surpassing all art ;
His joke sometimes carried reproof to a clown.

" A way of his own," is an idiomatic phrase often heard in Ireland, and employed very much as the French use " *Je ne sais quoi.*" As for a joke carrying reproof, that is a common mode of fence in Ireland, and no one understands it better than the Irish priest, himself a Celt, and "to the manner born;" and many a tough fellow that would stand without flinching under a battery of serious rebuke, will wince under a witticism.

Note 13—Page 35.

Griddle bread.

The domestic utensil called "griddle" in Ireland, goes by the name of "girdle" in Scotland, and is so spelt in Johnson's dictionary, with the definition "a round iron plate for baking." The griddle bread of Ireland is a flat cake of about an inch and a half in thickness, generally made of whole wheaten meal mixed with water and without yeast.

Note 14—Page 38.

The hypocrite penitent cunningly found
This means of suppressing suspicion around.
Would the murderer of Frank e'er confess to his brother?

Here was a very crafty culprit; for while to the senses of the world in general it would appear impossible that the murderer would have chosen the brother of his victim for his confessor, yet that very act was the surest to paralyze the action of the person most interested in making a discovery, for even if any chance had afterwards thrown in the priest's way a clue to the mystery, yet he, having been already entrusted with the fatal secret under "the solemn seal of confession," was precluded from making any use of it, as a word, or a look of his, indicating or suggesting even a suspicion in the true direction, would have been a violation of the sacred trust reposed in him. The priest was, in fact, as the last line of the stanza states, committed "To *silent* knowledge of guilty deed."

NOTE 15—Page 42.

But now the sun,
The daylight hears what thine arm hath done.

The moment the culprit made an *open declaration* of having committed murder, his words reached the ear of the priest under a new condition, and left him a free agent to publish the guilt.

--- —

THE BLACKSMITH.

NOTE 16—Page 50.

In the dead of the night loaded arms he conceal'd
In the ridge of potatoes in Phaidrig's own field.

The concealment of arms, or any other thing that involved a violation of the law, was not uncommonly resorted to by informers of the period to which this story refers. The rigorous enactments of those days, and the unscrupulous manner in which they were carried out, offered tempting opportunities to any miscreant to inculpate an innocent man.

NOTE 17—Page 51.

Then ready unfurled was the transport ship's sail,
To hurry the doom'd beyond respite or hope.

This is no exaggeration. In those days of "Whiteboy Prosecutions," the condemned were sent direct from the court-house dock on board the transport, with a view to strike terror through the land. In *these* days, it is often found difficult to obtain a conviction even for murder; and should conviction *be* obtained, even then, with verdict recorded and sentence passed, we have seen appeal made for mercy. But at the period to which our tale refers, many an innocent man was "whistled down the wind" to the penal colonies.

NOTE 18—Page 53.

And then rose the Judge's mild voice.

"Transportation" the sentence—but softly 't was said
(Like the summer wind waving the grass o'er the dead).

Such judges have been; in whom the *suaviter in modo, fortiter in re*, has rendered their sentences but more terrible.

NOTE 19—Page 54.

Heav'n hears the pray'r of the innocent breath;
Since the poor boy's not plazed with the sintence they found,
Maybe God will be good to him—and he'll be dhrown'd!

This passage may seem grotesque to the English reader, but not to those conversant with Ireland. In the first place, there is a deep trust amongst the

Irish people that "the prayer of the innocent" is never unavailing. In the second, the phrase "God will be good to him," is not of the author's making, but a national form of speech; and that a grant of Divine *favour* should be inferred from the anticipated fact of a man being *drowned*, is but one of those grotesque figures of speech that Ireland abounds in, but which, on investigation, and taken with the context, will be found to contain this meaning—that Heaven will grant the prayer of injured innocence.

Note 20—Page 56.

That warning so terrible—Vengeance is mine.

"For it is written, Vengeance is mine, I will repay, saith the Lord."— *Romans* xii. 19.

MISCELLANEOUS POEMS.

Note 21—Page 103.

While the dove of the deluge is over our roof.

The banks of the Mississippi are for the greater part singularly low, in consequence of which, floodings of a fearful nature often take place throughout the forests along its margin. The lines to which this note refers were suggested by my witnessing such an inroad where two or three log-huts, in the midst of the flooded wilderness, hundreds of miles away from any town, awakened a sense of imminent danger and desolate helplessness, that was absolutely painful. The vast sweep of the waters was sufficient to remind one of the days of Noah, and there was, in fact, a dovecot perched on the stump of a water-willow close by the gable of one of the houses, to complete the association of ideas.

NOTE 22—Page 104.

With thy emerald robe flowing brightly and free.

The brilliant green of the water as it flows in its greatest volume over the centre of the Horse-shoe Fall, is among the many beauties that render renowned this matchless cataract.

NOTE 23—Page 106.

The Flower of Night.

The Singadi, or Night-Tree of Sumatra, puts forth flowers at sunset and throughout the night, which fade after sunrise.

LONDON:
HENRY VIZETELLY, PRINTER AND ENGRAVER,
GOUGH SQUARE, FLEET STREET.